Copyright © 1978 by Intercontinental Book Productions.
Printed in the United States of America
by Rand McNally & Company. 1983 Edition.
Library of Congress Catalog Card Number: 83-61136

Emerald Fairy Tales

GEM CLASSICS LIBRARY

Retold by Jane Carruth

RAND McNALLY & COMPANY

Chicago • New York • San Francisco

Contents

Snow White and the Seven Dwarfs

IN THE snowy depths of winter, a long, long time ago, a fair and gentle Queen sat sewing by her window. As she stitched, her thoughts were far away from her work, so that suddenly she pricked her finger. A single drop of blood stained the snow on the window-sill and it was followed by another and then another. The Queen stared down at them wistfully.

"Ah," she thought, putting aside her sewing, "if only I had a child as white as this snow, with cheeks as red as this blood, and with hair as black as the ebony of this window-frame."

Shortly afterwards a little daughter was born to the Queen, and her skin was indeed as white as snow, her cheeks as red as blood and her hair as black as ebony. The Queen named her Snow-White.

Alas, after only a few short years, the gentle Queen died and the King, in his loneliness and grief, made up his mind to marry again.

But this time he chose unwisely, for his new wife, though very beautiful, was proud and cruel. Her greatest fear was that there should be anyone more beautiful than herself.

Her most treasured possession was an enchanted mirror which, when she stood before it, would answer any question she asked.

"Oh, mirror, mirror on the wall,
Who is the fairest of us all?"

she would ask of it. And the mirror would reply,

"You are the fairest, Lady Queen."

This reply would delight the haughty Queen for she knew her mirror could not lie to her.

But now Snow-White was growing up and with the passing years she was becoming prettier and prettier. Her beauty became so noticeable that even the humblest kitchen-maid, at work in the palace kitchens, would whisper, "Our young mistress is becoming far lovelier than our proud Queen."

One day the Queen asked her mirror,

"Oh, mirror, mirror on the wall,
Who is the fairest of us all?"

She waited haughtily for the mirror's answer and it replied,

"You were the fairest, Lady Queen.
Now Snow-White is the fairest seen."

The Queen's face turned green with jealousy when she heard this and her hatred for poor Snow-White knew no bounds. From that moment she determined to destroy the girl, but how could she do it? Snow-White was a King's daughter and the Queen did not dare show her hatred for the gentle Princess. She had in her employ, however, a huntsman whom she thought she could trust, so she sent for him.

"Take Snow-White into the forest," she told him, "and kill her! And prove to me that you have done this deed by bringing me back her heart and her tongue. Then I will know she is dead."

The huntsman was horrified at the Queen's command but he was so frightened of her and of what she might do if he defied her that he promised to do as she commanded. That same afternoon, he took Snow-White deep into the forest and, in a wild and lonely spot, he drew out his hunting knife.

"It is the Queen's command," he told her sorrowfully. "If I do not kill you, she will have me killed."

Tearfully Snow-White begged for her life. "Spare me!" she cried, "spare me, and I will live in the forest. I will never return to the palace, I promise, and the Queen will think I am dead."

So beautiful did she look and so piteously did she plead that the huntsman's heart was touched. "I will kill a wild boar," he said at last, "and take its tongue and heart back to the Queen. Pray God that she will be deceived."

In her gratitude, Snow-White kissed the huntsman's rough hand and fled from him deeper into the forest. True to his word, the hunter caught and killed a wild boar and took from it the tongue and heart. These he showed to the Queen on his return to the palace. She smiled cruelly, her hard eyes glinting, and then she gave him a bag of gold for his pains.

"At last," she thought, "I have rid myself of the girl and no one will guess how or why she has vanished from the palace!"

But what of Snow-White? Alone in the gloomy forest, she was at first filled with terror, for she knew there were wild beasts around who might harm her. But as she ran over the grass and through thorn bushes that tore her clothes no wild beasts attacked her; they saw her, but they did not touch her. How far she had covered in her headlong flight or where she was, she had no idea, but just as it was growing dark she came upon a little house.

"I will ask for shelter," Snow-White decided. "Whoever lives here surely cannot refuse me that."

When no one answered her knock, she pushed against the door and found it was not locked. So, timidly, she went into the cottage. It was very small, but oh, so neat and tidy that Snow-White clapped her hands.

She saw, in the middle of the room, a little table covered with a sparkling white cloth. The table was set with seven little plates and beside each plate was a knife and fork. There were also seven little mugs with seven little spoons set neatly beside them. Against the walls were seven little beds, each covered with a different-colored counterpane.

Snow-White cut herself a thin slice of bread and took a tiny piece of meat from each of the plates. Then she sipped something that tasted like sweet apple juice from one of the mugs. After that she was so tired that she lay down on one of the beds and was soon fast asleep.

Now this cottage belonged to seven little dwarfs who worked all day in the mountains – mining gold and ore. Imagine their surprise when they came home that night and found a young girl fast asleep on one of their beds.

"How pretty she is!" they exclaimed, holding up their lanterns so that they could see Snow-White more clearly. "And how soundly she sleeps!"

Then the seventh little man said, "It would be a shame to disturb her. Let her sleep on. We will ask her who she is and how she found her way here in the morning."

As soon as dawn broke, Snow-White woke up from her slumbers. The sight of the seven little men around her bed instantly frightened her, but they smiled at her so kindly that she managed to smile back. And then they began to question her.

"Who are you?"

"Where do you come from?"

"What are you doing here?"

Snow-White took a deep breath and told them about the wicked Queen, her stepmother. And then about the kind-hearted huntsman and how she had stumbled upon their cottage.

The little men listened attentively. Then they said, "You can make your home with us now, for it is plain you must never return to the palace. And if you will promise to take care of us, clean and cook and knit for us, we will see that you want for nothing."

"That is just what I should love to do!" Snow-White cried happily. "I promise I will take good care of you all."

So the dwarfs went off to work in the mountains and in their absence, Snow-White busied herself about the cottage, polishing and dusting. Then she cooked a tasty meal for them so that when they came home, tired and hungry, they would have something delicious to eat.

"We have made a very good bargain," said the seventh little man that night, as he and the others sat down at the table. "You are an excellent cook, Snow-White."

"We hope you will stay with us forever," said the others, and Snow-White smiled. The kind little dwarfs had won her heart.

So the days passed happily. Snow-White darned and knitted and sewed when all the housework was done and she kept herself so busy that she never felt lonely. But the dwarfs often spoke about her wicked stepmother and warned her that one day the Queen might seek her out and try once again to have her killed.

Meanwhile, the Queen was content. She was so certain that her hated rival was dead that she did not bother to speak to her magic mirror for many weeks. Then, one day, when she found herself in

the secret room at the top of the palace where she kept the mirror,
she stood before it and almost without thinking said,

"Oh, mirror, mirror on the wall,
Who is the fairest of us all?"
And the mirror replied,

"You were the fairest, Lady Queen,
Now Snow-White is the fairest seen.
Amid the forest, darkly green,
She lives with seven dwarfs, I ween."

The Queen was stricken with fury when she heard this. She
knew that the mirror could speak only the truth and that therefore
the huntsman had deceived her.

Day and night she thought of how she might destroy Snow-
White and, at last, a plan came to her. Without more delay, she
stained her face with dye and borrowed clothes belonging to an old
peddler woman. In this disguise she made her way through the
forest until she came to the cottage of the seven dwarfs. Then she
knocked at the door.

"Beautiful, colored laces for sale!" she called out when she saw

Snow-White's face at the window. "Come out, dearie, and buy some to match your pretty eyes."

"My dwarfs do not like me speaking to strangers," said Snow-White. "But I am sure they would want me to have some of these pretty laces. Wait a minute and I will come to the door."

"Here is a pretty blue pair," said the peddler woman when Snow-White stood before her. "Let me lace up your bodice with them."

And Snow-White, suspecting nothing, let the old woman thread the laces through her bodice. But the Queen pulled the laces so tightly that the girl lost all her breath and fell down on the step as if dead. With an evil chuckle, the wicked Queen ran into the forest.

Luckily, the dwarfs came home early that day from the mines. When they saw Snow-White lying so still before their cottage door, they were terribly frightened.

"Hold her head!" cried one.

"Let me cut these tight laces," cried another.

When this was done, Snow-White slowly began to breathe again and the dwarfs shouted for joy. Then they carried her inside and laid her gently on one of the beds.

"Who gave you the laces?" they asked Snow-White anxiously.

And Snow-White told them about the old peddler woman.

"She was your evil stepmother in disguise," said the seventh dwarf. "And when she finds out that you are still alive she will try again. So be warned, Snow-White. You must not open the door to anyone when we are away working in the mines."

Now no sooner was the Queen back in the palace than she went to her mirror and asked,

"Oh, mirror, mirror on the wall,
Who is the fairest of us all?"

And the mirror replied,

"You were the fairest, Lady Queen.
Now Snow-White is the fairest seen."

The Queen knew that her plan had failed, and she turned green and purple with envy and rage as she stamped her feet on the floor.

Again she thought and thought of how she might destroy the girl and, at last, another plan came to her. Using her wicked powers,

she made a poisoned comb. Then disguising herself as a jolly peasant woman, she set off through the forest until she once more came to the dwarfs' cottage.

As she knocked at the door, she called out, "I have some pretty combs to sell. Look at this one, did you ever see such a beauty!"

Snow-White, who had been peeping at her from the window, exclaimed, "Oh, I would love to wear such a comb! How it sparkles in the sunshine! But I cannot come out . . ."

"It will take only a second for me to fix this pretty comb in your lovely black hair," wheedled the old peasant woman. "Just open the door."

And Snow-White allowed herself to be persuaded. She opened the door, and the woman drew the poisoned comb through her long hair. But scarcely had she done so than the poison began to work, and Snow-White fell down senseless. The Queen stared down at her for a moment and then ran into the forest.

Once again the dwarfs came home earlier than usual that day and when they saw Snow-White lying there with the comb still in her hair, they drew it out immediately and carried her indoors.

"We are not too late!" cried one of the dwarfs. "She is opening her eyes. The poison has not had time to do its evil work."

When Snow-White was stronger she told them about the kindly old peasant woman. The dwarfs scolded her a little.

"You must not open the door again," they told her as firmly as they could. "Your stepmother will try again, be sure of that."

The dwarfs were right, for it did not take the Queen long to find out from her magic mirror that Snow-White was still alive. This time she used her powers to make a poisoned apple. So beautiful was it and so inviting that no one could ever have guessed that one half of the apple was filled with the most deadly poison.

Satisfied that no power on earth could save Snow-White once she had tasted the apple, the wicked Queen disguised herself once more – this time as a plump, white-haired old farmer's wife – and set off through the forest.

"I cannot come out!" Snow-White called through the window when she saw the old woman. "I have promised my dwarfs that I will answer the door to no one."

"Ah, but there is no need for you to come to the door," said the old woman, holding up the rosy-cheeked apple. "I will stand beneath your window and hand it up to you."

Snow-White opened the window but still she hesitated, and the woman cried, "Do not be afraid of the apple. Look, I will take a bite from one side."

Snow-White watched while she did so and she thought, "Oh, it looks so delicious. Surely it cannot harm me!"

"Give me a taste of the apple, old woman," she said suddenly. And she reached down and took the apple. But scarcely had she taken a bite than she fell to the floor – dead.

The Queen laughed harshly when she saw her fall. Then she exclaimed, "White as snow, red as blood, black as ebony! This time the dwarfs will never bring you back to life." And she ran from the cottage and disappeared into the forest. When she was back in the palace, she went immediately to her mirror and said,

"Oh, mirror, mirror on the wall,
Who is the fairest of us all?"
And this time the mirror answered,
"You are the fairest, Lady Queen."
The Queen's jealousy was settled and she forgot Snow-White.

The grief the little dwarfs suffered when they found Snow-White lying dead on their cottage floor was terrible to see. They knew that, at last, her stepmother had defeated them. Snow-White was dead and they knew they could never bring her back to life. Sadly, they washed her pretty face and hands and dressed her hair with flowers. She seemed to them even more beautiful in death than she had been in life.

"She is too lovely to bury in the cold, dark earth," one little man said. "Let us place her in a glass coffin for all the world to see."

And when this was done, the seventh dwarf wrote her name on the glass in gold letters. Then underneath it he put the words: "A King's Daughter."

The little men placed the glass coffin on a flat rock just outside their garden gate and they mounted guard over it so that now only six dwarfs went off to work in the mines while one always stayed with the coffin.

For many months Snow-White lay in her glass case in the forest and she remained as lovely as she had been when she was alive. Her skin was as white as snow, her lips as red as blood and her hair the color of ebony. Then one day a young, handsome Prince came riding through the forest with his attendants. He saw the girl and thought for a moment she was asleep.

"She is not sleeping," the dwarf on guard told him mournfully. "She is dead, alas!"

The Prince gazed long and earnestly at the beautiful girl; he stayed all that day by the glass case and in the evening he went to the dwarfs' cottage.

"Let me take the coffin back with me to my own kingdom," he said. "I cannot bear to leave that lovely girl here in the forest."

And when the dwarfs refused his request, he offered them gold.

"She is not for sale," said the seventh dwarf angrily. And the Prince turned sadly away. But he could not leave the forest and, as the days passed, the dwarfs came to understand that the Prince loved Snow-White almost as much as they did.

One morning they told him, "You may carry our Snow-White back to your own kingdom. It is perhaps selfish of us to keep her here in the silent forest. Her beauty should be known to the wide world."

Overjoyed, the Prince ordered his attendants to pick up the glass case. But as they carried it away on their shoulders one of them caught his foot in the root of a tree and stumbled. The coffin tilted and the piece of poisoned apple, which had been lodged in Snow-White's throat, fell from her mouth. Almost at once, she opened her eyes. Then she raised the lid of the glass case and sat up.

Too astonished to speak, the Prince rushed towards her and helped her out of the case. Then he took her in his arms and told her of his love for her. But it was to the kind little dwarfs that Snow-

White turned and, overjoyed, they led her into the cottage and told her all that happened.

What happiness and merriment there was in the cottage that day! The Prince was as joyful as the dwarfs for Snow-White had consented to ride away with him and be his wife.

"But only on one condition," she said firmly, "and that is that my seven dwarfs are invited to our wedding."

So the Prince won for his bride the beautiful Snow-White and the wedding was celebrated with magnificent pomp and ceremony. But in the eyes of Snow-White the most important guests of all were her beloved little dwarfs.

News of such a grand affair soon reached the ears of the wicked Queen. At first she would not believe that the Prince's bride could be Snow-White. But when her magic mirror told her that the fairest in the land was the Prince's bride, she knew beyond doubt that Snow-White still lived.

And as she stood there before her mirror – trembling with rage – the envy and spite which filled her heart spilled over and she began to smolder and then burn. Soon there was nothing left of her but a heap of gray ashes. The dwarfs of course had nothing to do with this, but somehow they found out about it and were able to tell Snow-White that no longer need she fear the wicked Queen.

The White Dove

O NCE UPON a time a King had two sons who were so
daring and reckless that they never gave him a moment's
freedom from worry. Every day they would think of
something new and dangerous to do. Already they had scaled the
highest mountains, hunted the most ferocious tigers and ridden the
wildest horses in the land. But still they were not satisfied.

One day, the brothers went to the King.

"Father, we have not yet sailed the sea in a storm," said one.

"We have a great desire to do this," said the other. "It would be a
new kind of adventure for us."

The King was horrified. "But you are not sailors," he protested.
"You have never handled a boat and if you capsize there will be no
one to save you."

His sons laughed merrily at the idea of such a catastrophe and the
King, knowing that it would be useless to argue with the brothers,
had no alternative but to let them go.

As usual the young men made no preparation for their new
adventure. They just mounted their horses and rode down to the

sea, choosing a lonely, deserted part of the coast. Then they searched around until they found an old boat that had belonged to a fisherman. It was lying deserted on the beach.

"This boat will serve our purpose very well," said the elder brother. "And if it leaks, well – it will make our adventure all the more exciting!"

They waited until the sky grew dark with threatening clouds and the wind began blustering and bullying the foam-crested waves.

"Time, I think, to launch our boat," cried Edgar, the younger of the brothers. "Come on!"

They rowed their old boat out to sea in the very teeth of the wind. A storm of rain beat down on them, soaking their colored tunics. Then as the sky grew black with thunder clouds and the storm broke in all its fury, their little boat sprung a leak.

"Can you swim, brother?" asked Edgar, still able to smile as he began bailing out water furiously.

"Never a stroke," replied his brother. "And I have no great wish to end my days at the bottom of the sea."

"Nor I," said Edgar. Then he added seriously, "But for once, I

think we have taken on an adventure that is going to send us to our doom."

Just when the two brothers had resolved to die as bravely as they had lived, they saw, riding over the mountainous waves, a strange tub-like vessel made out of stone. In it sat an old crone whose long, wispy hair blew wildly in the wind. She was using a spade to steer her tub and so deftly did she handle it, she was soon alongside.

"What will you give me," she screeched, above the noise of the storm, "if I take you back to safety?"

"Anything!" Edgar shouted. "Anything you care to ask for."

"We are the sons of a King," his brother added. "Our father will see to it that you are well rewarded."

"I want neither gold nor silver," replied the old witch, for that was what she was.

"Then what do you want?" demanded Edgar. "If you don't tell us quickly we will no longer be here to bargain with you!"

"Promise me," said the witch, "Promise me that I will get your lady mother's next child. Promise on your sacred word that when I come for him he will be given to me!"

"Never!" exclaimed the two brothers together.

25

Then, as their boat sank deeper into the waves, Edgar cried, "Oh, very well, we give you our word. But, our mother is long past the age for bearing children. You have made a bad bargain!"

"Jump into my tub," said the witch, ignoring this remark, and, holding out the spade, she pulled him into the tub beside her. Then, having done the same for his brother, she rowed her strange craft over the angry waves towards the distant shore.

As soon as the brothers found themselves on dry land, they thanked the old hag and went to where they had tethered their horses. Then, with no more delay, they galloped back to the palace.

They said nothing of their adventure to the King, but, from that time onwards, they behaved rather more soberly. Often, when they found themselves on their own together, they would talk about the old hag who had saved them from a watery grave.

"Our mother is too old to have another child. We have fooled the old witch and as she wanted none of our gold we are not likely to see her again," one would say to the other.

But the brothers were wrong in thinking that their mother would not have another child, for a year later a fine baby boy was born to her. The brothers were so alarmed that they mounted guard over the new young prince and scarcely ever stirred from his side.

So the years passed. The King grew feeble and became unable to lead his army against the many people that threatened his kingdom.

Soon the country was at war and the two brothers, although they were unhappy to leave their charge, prepared to ride into battle.

"Our young brother is old enough now to take care of himself," said Edgar. "He can ride and shoot almost as skillfully as we can. There should be no danger in leaving him."

So the brothers rode off, but, sad to say, were killed in battle, although they had fought most gallantly.

Meanwhile – at home at the palace – the young prince practiced all the arts of warfare and combat his brothers had taught him. He longed for their return so that he could show them how well he had progressed. But they did not appear. Instead, one day, at the height of a terrible storm, the old witch came to the palace.

She found the prince in the stables where he was endeavoring to quiet the panicking horses. Pointing a long skinny finger at him, she croaked, "You are mine! I have come to claim you!"

At first the boy laughed, thinking that the old woman – whoever she was – had taken leave of her senses.

"Why should I go with you?" he demanded. "My place is here in the palace. One day I may be King."

"Your place is at my side," croaked the old witch. "Your two brothers promised you to me on the night of a terrible storm. A promise – particularly a royal promise – may not be broken."

With that, she took hold of the boy's arm and led him out of the stables, across the deserted courtyard and away from the palace. No matter how hard he struggled, the young prince found he could not break away from her grasp.

Over hills and fields and through dark forests they went, until at last they came to the sea. There, on the shore, was the witch's tub.

"Now you will sail with me," she cackled, "as did once those reckless brothers of yours."

Powerless to resist her, the prince boarded the tub as it bobbed up and down in the water. The witch hopped in beside him, picking up the spade to steer the craft. How long they sailed or how they survived the fierce storm that was raging, the boy had no inkling. But as they raced along he was suddenly overcome by sleep. And the witch, on seeing his eyes close, gave an evil chuckle.

When the prince awoke from his enchanted sleep, he found he was no longer in the tub but in a large room with windows that looked out over the sea. He saw the witch watching him from the doorway, and he shouted, "Let me go, you old crone! My father is a King – he will soon send soldiers to find me."

"You have but one task in which to fail, and then you will be mine forever," said the witch, ignoring his remarks as she dragged a sack into the room. "Pick it up, my young cock, and shake it well."

The boy obeyed and immediately the room was thick with feathers. They floated all around him some settling on his face, some on his hands, and some on his shoulders. For every one he brushed away, another took its place.

"The feathers must be returned to the sack by nightfall," said the witch with a crafty smile.

"That's an impossible task!" the prince cried. "Why, there are thousands of feathers and . . ." But the witch had gone.

He began at once to try and catch the feathers but they floated away from him as if they had a life of their own. On seeing the hopelessness of his task, the prince gave up trying to catch them and sat down, burying his face in his hands. As he sat there wondering

what to do next, he heard a tapping on the window and looking up he saw a beautiful white dove.

He opened the window and the bird flew into the room. Without a word, it set to work to pick up all the feathers, putting each one in the sack, and, by nightfall, the dove had accomplished the task.

Filled with gratitude, the prince stroked the beautiful white bird and then impulsively kissed its silky head as he held it gently in his hands. Straightaway, the bird changed into a wonderfully pretty young girl with raven black hair and eyes as blue as cornflowers.

"I, too, am in the witch's power," she told him. "But if you promise to do what I tell you, we may yet both be free of her enchantment."

"What is it I must do?" whispered the prince. "How long before you change back into a dove again?"

"At daybreak," the girl told him sadly. "But listen carefully. When the old witch comes and finds that you have performed her task, she will hide her rage and disappointment. She will ask you to stay with her of your own free will to take care of her. You must pretend to agree. Then ask her immediately to grant you a wish."

"What kind of a wish?" demanded the prince. "I can think of only how much I wish that you were free of her wicked spell."

"Ask her for the princess that flies about as a white dove," was the reply.

Then the girl took from the pocket of her dress a length of red silk thread and gave it to the prince.

"Wind this tightly round my little finger," she said, "so that whatever the old witch does, you will recognize me by it."

The Prince did as she asked just as the first light of morning crept across the sky. Immediately the lovely girl changed into the white dove and straightaway flew out of the window. At almost exactly the same time, the witch appeared and when she saw the sack filled to the brim with feathers, she hid her disappointment — just as the princess had said she would.

"Well, mother," said the prince cheerfully. "I have completed the task you set me. May I return to my father's kingdom?"

"Stay with me of your own free will," wheedled the witch. "Stay and take care of me in my old age and I will give you riches beyond your dreams."

The prince nodded as if he might well consider her offer. Then he said quickly, "As proof of your good intentions, give me the princess that flies about as a white dove."

A wicked, crafty look came into the witch's red eyes. Then she said sweetly, "I know nothing of a white dove and there is no princess here. But you may have my little gray donkey."

She took the prince out of the house and into the woods. There she showed him a little donkey that was standing quietly eating the grass. The prince was about to refuse her gift with all the dignity he could muster when, suddenly, he saw, wound round the donkey's hoof, the thin, red, silken thread.

"Thank you," he said. "I will take the little gray donkey."

At this the witch's face grew grim and her eyes darkened. She snatched up a stick and beat the donkey savagely with it, driving it away into the woods. As the prince waited, the witch soon returned, muttering to herself and dragging along a toothless old nag. This she offered to the Prince.

Just as he was about to refuse such a poor substitute for the pretty donkey, he saw around its tail the red silken thread. "Thank you," he said. "I will take the old nag and ride·it for my pleasure."

As the nag changed at once into the lovely Princess the witch knew her power over the two young people was broken. Shaking her skinny fist at them, she gave a melancholy shriek and ran down towards the sea. Without a moment's hesitation she plunged into the gray water and was swallowed up by a huge wave.

As so frequently happens in true fairy stories, the prince found his own way home to the palace, with the princess at his side. They were married within the year at the old King's request and there was no happier couple in all the land!

The Little Drummer Boy

ONCE UPON a time there lived a brave Drummer-boy who dreamed every day about fighting in great battles. But there was peace in the land and the Drummer-boy could find no way to prove his courage.

One day, as he was wandering through the woods, he came upon a deep pool. Lying at the water's edge were three pieces of fine white linen.

"What beautiful linen," he said to himself. "It seems a shame to leave it here by this pool." And he picked up one of the pieces and took it home with him.

The Drummer-boy soon forgot all about the linen, but that night, as he lay in bed, he heard a gentle voice calling him.

"Drummer-boy, Drummer-boy," said the voice, "give me back my linen-wrap."

The Drummer-boy sat up in his bed. The room was dark but it seemed to him that the ghostly shape of a girl was floating up and down close to his bed.

"Who are you?" he asked. "And why do you want the linen?"

"I am a Princess," the voice said, "and I am bound forever to a wicked witch. Each day my sisters and I must bathe in the pool you came across today. When we wrap the linen about us we can fly back to our palace for just two hours."

"What happens then?" asked the Drummer-boy, pinching himself under the bedclothes to make sure he was truly awake.

"As I am the eldest," replied the Princess, "I have to return to the Glass Mountain where the old witch lives. There she keeps me a prisoner."

"I have never heard of such things before," cried the Drummer-boy jumping out of bed. "Of course – you must have your linen-wrap." He crossed the floor to a cupboard and took out the cloth, which he handed to the ghostly maiden.

She accepted it thankfully, but the Drummer-boy cried, "Don't fly away now that you have what you came for. Stay a moment longer, for I would like to hear if I can help you."

"There is no way you can help me," answered the girl faintly. "No mortal man has yet succeeded in climbing the Glass Mountain, Drummer-boy, and even if you did succeed, the wicked witch would be waiting for you."

"It is true I know nothing of the Glass Mountain," said the Drummer-boy. "But I have a stout heart and a determination that longs for adventure. If you tell me the road I must follow to find it, I will set out in the morning."

"The road passes through a vast forest," said the voice. "Where man-eating giants live – it is truly a frightening place and . . ."

The voice faded away and the Drummer-boy cried, "Don't go yet! Tell me more!" But the ghostly figure was no longer there and the Drummer-boy was soon dreaming of giants and witches.

At the first light of morning the Drummer-boy jumped from his bed, slung his drum across his back and set out down the road. When he came to the forest he entered it fearlessly, but of giants there was neither sight nor sound.

"If they will not seek me out," he thought, "then I must seek them." So he took his drum and beat a loud tattoo upon it. As the roll of his drum echoed through the forest the huge figure of a giant rose up from the long grass where he had previously been fast asleep. Tall and strong as an oak tree, he was a terrible sight and all the more frightening because his huge face was lined and pitted as if it had been struck by iron hailstones.

When the giant caught sight of the tiny Drummer-boy, he roared, "Ho-there, beetle, what do you mean by disturbing my sleep with all that drumming?"

"I meant no harm," said the Drummer-boy. "The roll of my drum was to tell the regiment that I had found a giant."

"What do you mean – found a giant?" demanded the giant.

"My regiment has come to the forest to rid the King of the land of all you giants," said the Drummer-boy quietly. "You should see them – only I don't suppose you will. Anyway, they will soon be here; thousands of them, wearing helmets of steel and suits of shiny armor the like of which has never been seen before. They fight with the cunning of demons, and they mean to capture you and others like you before nightfall."

In spite of himself the giant was impressed. "Why don't you suppose I will see them if they will soon be here?" he asked.

"Because they are small, like me," said the Drummer-boy. "They will advance on you by stealth. They will creep up on you with their cords of steel and their steel hammers and before you know it, they will bring you crashing to the ground. Then they will bind your eyes as well as your hands and feet . . ."

A startled look came into the giant's eyes. He would be no match

against thousands of invisible demon-soldiers, wearing steel helmets, their cords of steel ready to bind his arms and legs.

"You say they are already advancing?" he asked apprehensively after another silence.

"They are," replied the Drummer-boy confidently. "My drum has told them that I have found a giant."

"I suppose you couldn't make that drum of yours tell them the exact opposite, could you?" asked the giant.

"Of course! I can make my drum tell them anything I want to!" replied the Drummer-boy.

"Then you could send all the soldiers away – right away from this part of the forest," said the giant. "Would you do that?"

The Drummer-boy pretended to be doubtful.

"I'll – I'll do anything, absolutely anything you want," offered the giant becoming even more nervous. "Just say what you want and I'll do it."

"Well," began the Drummer-boy, "in that case – perhaps I could do such a favor for you. Yes, I will." And he unslung his drum and made as if to beat it.

"Ah!" he began again. "Ah yes, but first I must ask if you will carry me to the Glass Mountain. If you will, then I'll make my drum speak."

"Certainly, of course." The giant was so frightened that he was actually kneeling before the little Drummer-boy.

"That's good," said the Drummer-boy. "I'll get there faster in that case for your legs are much longer than mine." And he began beating loudly on his drum. "Now, my soldiers will not come this way," he said when he had finished.

Greatly relieved, the giant picked up the Drummer-boy, seated him on his shoulder and set off through the forest.

"What is this Glass Mountain?" asked the Drummer-boy, as they sped along.

"It's three times as high as the highest mountain you can imagine and it's so slippery that not even a bird could land there," grunted the giant. "No man has ever climbed it."

But no matter what the giant said about the Glass Mountain, the Drummer-boy refused to be downcast. When, at last, the giant set him down at its foot, he thanked him warmly.

For a long time the Drummer-boy stared up at the Glass Mountain and slowly, as darkness began to fall, he realized that he could never climb it without help. As slippery as his looking-glass at home, the Mountain was everything the giant had said about it. It simply could not be climbed. Then and only then did the little Drummer-boy begin to feel sad and weary. If he could not conquer the Glass Mountain, he would not see the beautiful girl ever again.

As he stood there, bruised and discouraged from the many attempts he had already made to climb the slippery slope, two men came into view. They were, it seemed, in the middle of a violent quarrel and the Drummer-boy walked towards them.

"You will come to blows soon," he told them, "if you do not stop cursing each other. What is it you fight about so bitterly?"

"Keep out of this, boy," said one of the men roughly.

But the other pointed to an old saddle which lay on the ground between them.

"We are fighting for the saddle," said he. "And I assure you it is worth fighting for. Whoever sits on that saddle and wishes to be in a particular place – and it can be anywhere in the world – the saddle will carry him there in an instant."

"A flying saddle?" said the Drummer-boy, staring at the saddle with great interest. "No wonder that you are fighting over it!"

"We each took an equal share in winning it," said the first man. "Now we cannot decide which one of us should have it."

"It is mine!" shouted his companion.

"Stop!" cried the Drummer-boy. "Stop it! Listen to me. I know how to settle the argument for you." And walking away from the two men, he broke off the branch of a tree and stuck it into the ground.

"Now," said he, "settle it with a race. The first to reach this stick will be the first to ride the saddle."

The men agreed, but as they set off to race to the stick, the Drummer-boy swung himself into the saddle and wished that it might take him to the top of the Glass Mountain.

Before he had time to congratulate himself on how things had turned out, the Drummer-boy found himself at the top of the mountain. In front of him was a wide-open, flat space in which stood an old stone house.

Behind the old house stretched a dark and gloomy forest, and in front of it lay a large fish-pond.

The Drummer-boy, with the clouds floating just above his head, looked about him for any sight or sound of life but there was only the noise of the wind moaning eerily through the trees. And he thought to himself that this strange place was surely more frightening than any battlefield.

Whistling to keep up his courage, he went over to the old stone house and knocked.

The ancient crone who came to the door had red eyes and a pair of spectacles perched on the end of her long nose. The Drummer-boy knew at once that he was looking at a witch.

"What do you want here?" she croaked, and her eyes were sharp with spite as she peered at him.

"Nothing more than a night's shelter, ma'am, and a bite to eat," the Drummer-boy replied boldly enough.

"You are welcome to both," replied the old witch. "But in return, tomorrow you must ladle the water out of the fish-pond and lay the fish you find there side by side, according to their kind. This you must do by nightfall."

"I understand," said the Drummer-boy, and entered the house.

The witch fed him well and gave him a soft bed in which to sleep. The Drummer-boy slept soundly but, by early morning, he was wide awake and ready to perform his task.

"Give me a large bucket, mother," he called out cheerfully.

"Take this," said the witch with a spiteful cackle, and she handed him a silver thimble she pulled from her withered finger. "You must use this thimble to empty the pond."

41

The Drummer-boy labored all morning at the pond knowing in his heart that the task was impossible. "If I had a thousand years or more to empty this pond of all its water, I could not succeed with just a thimble," he said to himself.

And sighing wearily, he threw the thimble away and sat down by the water's edge. At midday, the door of the little house opened and out came a beautiful young girl. The Drummer-boy took her for a poor serving maid for she was dressed in rags and her feet were bare. She carried a basket of food and set it down before him.

"You look so sad and tired. Why are you miserable?"

"The old witch has set me an impossible task," the Drummer-boy told her, with another deep sigh. "I came here to help a King's daughter but now it looks as if I have failed."

"I will help you," said the girl. "Put your head in my lap and go to sleep. When you awake, the fish-pond will be empty of water."

The Drummer-boy was too tired to ask any questions; with a smile of contentment he did as he was told and was soon fast asleep. As he slept, the girl twisted the strangely fashioned wishing-ring which she wore on a silver chain beneath her rags and murmured, "Water up! Fish out!"

At once the water in the pond spouted into the air and floated away like soft white mist. And the fish jumped onto the bank.

No wonder the Drummer-boy rubbed his eyes in astonishment when the girl roused him from his sleep for he saw that the pond was dry and the fish were lined up according to their size and species.

"All my work is done!" he cried in delight. "The witch can find no fault with this."

"Get up now," said the girl, "and put one of the fish by the tree there, away from its own kind . . ."

The Drummer-boy did this, and the girl continued, "When the witch comes at dusk you must throw this fish in her face with the words, 'This is for you, old witch!'"

"I will do it with pleasure," said the Drummer-boy. And with that the girl left him and went back into the house.

At dusk, the old witch reappeared; she said nothing at all about the empty pond but asked, "Why is that fish all by itself?"

Mindful of the girl's words, the Drummer-boy answered, "This is for you, old witch!" And then he threw the fish in her face.

The witch stood there for a moment as if nothing had happened.

Then she cried in a shrill, spiteful voice, "Ah, my soldier-boy, you have still much to do for me before you can leave this place. In the morning you must cut down the entire forest."

Early the next morning, the Drummer-boy went into the forest with the axe the witch had given him. But when he aimed a blow at the first tree he came to, the axe doubled up as if it were made of rubber. The Drummer-boy cast it away from him with disgust. "How can I work with such a tool?" he asked himself.

But just when his despair was at its height, the beautiful girl appeared before him.

"Lay your head in my lap," she said. "And I will awake you when the work is done."

So, once again, the Drummer-boy thankfully went to sleep. When his eyes were shut the girl turned her magic ring, saying, "Forest trees fall."

At once the great trees fell to the ground with a thunderous crashing that woke the Drummer-boy from his sleep.

"The witch will ask you to split the wood and lay the logs in bundles," said the girl. "But this, too, I will do for you."

"What other tasks has the witch in store for me?" asked the Drummer-boy. "What have I to do to overcome her?"

"When she comes at dusk, she will tell you to make a fire to warm her old bones. And when you have done this she will say, 'There is a log in the midst of the fire which will not burn, fetch it out for me!' If your heart is brave you will not be burned."

At dusk the old witch came into the forest where the trees were felled and neatly laid out in bundles.

"How cold it is tonight," she said, rubbing her hands together. "Make me a fire to warm my old bones."

The Drummer-boy obediently piled up the logs and soon had a huge fire roaring. But the witch was not satisfied. "I see in the midst of the flames a log which will not burn," she said. "Fetch it out for me and look sharp, soldier-boy!"

At once the Drummer-boy leaped into the flames and fetched out the log without so much as singeing one hair of his head! But no sooner had he laid the log at the witch's feet than it changed into the beautiful young girl who had performed each task for him. Now she was no longer dressed in rags but in a dress of shimmering silk embroidered with jewels, and on her head sat a golden crown.

"Yes," she said, "I am the Princess you came to save!"

Snarling with rage, her red eyes glowing with spite, the old witch tried to push the Princess back into the flames, but the Drummer-boy was too quick and too strong for her. He grasped her bodily in his arms and cast her into the flames, which immediately closed over her and devoured her.

"Her wicked spell is broken forever!" cried the Princess joyfully. "We are free to return home; my sisters will be with my father already for they, too, are now free of the enchantment."

"I have no wish to live in a King's palace," said the Drummer-boy, "but you are the only girl I would ever want to marry."

"Then I will come with you," said the Princess. "You have risked your life to set me free and the rest of it belongs to you."

The Drummer-boy seated her on his flying saddle and, climbing on behind, wished himself safely home.

Mindful of the fact that his parents were humble folk, the Drummer-boy asked his Princess if she would be willing to dress more suitably for her new way of life. And she gladly exchanged her golden crown and silken robe for a country girl's gown.

"She is so obedient to my slightest wish," he told himself. "I need have no fear that she will not make me a loving, devoted wife."

During the long, long years of happiness which followed, the Drummer-boy delighted in telling the story of the beautiful Princess and the Glass Mountain. But, sad to say, neither his children nor, when they grew up and married, his grandchildren believed there was any truth in the story. And this was mostly because he would not tell them where exactly the forest of giants was to be found, or where the Glass Mountain stood, or how it came about that a brave young Drummer-boy came face to face with a wicked, wicked witch.

Rumpelstiltskin

THERE WAS once a poor miller who always wanted to appear important in the eyes of all his friends. He had little to boast about except his only daughter, who was exceedingly pretty.

One day the miller found himself in the presence of the King. Now he was really at a loss, for he knew there was little sense in boasting about his house or his mill to a King who had everything. At last he blurted out, "I have a daughter, Your Majesty, a very pretty, clever child – so clever that she can spin straw into gold."

"That is a skill which I should like to possess," said the King. "Bring her to the palace tomorrow and if she is as clever as you say she is, I will reward you handsomely."

As you may imagine, the miller was in a rare fright when he got home, but wisely he said nothing of his boasting to his daughter. Instead he pretended to be very excited.

"Just think!" he told her. "The King wants to see you at the palace tomorrow. It is a great honor."

But the miller's daughter almost fainted away when she arrived at the palace the next day, for the King took her into a small room full of straw and pushed her towards a wheel and a shuttle.

"You must begin at once," he said. "You have everything you need to spin this straw into gold. If your task is not accomplished by morning, you shall be put to death."

Left alone, the miller's daughter buried her pretty head in her arms and began to sob bitterly. No one could spin straw into gold! This was an impossible task, yet if she did not do it, she would die.

At the height of her grief the door opened and into the room came a little man. He was so tiny that the girl did not even see him and went on sobbing.

But then he said, "Good day to you! Why do you weep so bitterly?" Well, that was a different matter!

The miller's daughter choked down her sobs and stared down in astonishment at the little goblin whose head seemed almost too big and heavy for the thin body and stick-like legs.

"I'll tell you why I am crying," she stammered. "And you would cry too if the King had commanded you to spin all this horrible straw into gold – that is what I must do and by the morning too!"

"That is too bad," said the little man, shaking his head. "Now what will you give me if I spin this straw into gold for you?"

"You may have my necklace," said the girl.

The little man took the necklace and sat down at the spinning wheel. In a few minutes the shuttle was full and he was spinning away at lightning speed. Then he filled another and another until, by early morning, there was not a piece of straw left; all of it was changed to gold.

Before the miller's daughter had time to thank the goblin he had vanished which was, perhaps, just as well for almost immediately afterwards the King appeared.

When he saw all the gold he praised the girl for her hard work. But being a greedy King he could think only of obtaining more. And he ordered the miller's daughter to be taken to a bigger room in which was stacked much more straw.

The girl's despair once again reduced her to bitter tears. She was sobbing as if her poor heart would break when the door suddenly opened and in came the little man again. "What will you give me this time if I spin all this straw into gold for you?" he asked.

The girl replied at once, "I will give you this gold ring. See how

49

pretty it is." And she pulled it off her finger and gave it to him.

The little man took the ring and sat down at the spinning wheel. By morning, he had spun all the straw into gold.

The King was extremely pleased when he came to see the miller's daughter the next morning. But still he wasn't satisfied; the sight of all that gold made him long for an even greater fortune.

He led the girl into a room which was twice the size of the one where she had spent the previous night. His servants carried great bundles of straw into the room and when it was filled, the King said, "If you spin all this straw into gold by daybreak, I will make you my wife."

"You mean I shall be a Queen?" asked the girl, forgetting in her excitement the task which she must first perform.

"I do," said the King, thinking to himself that he could do a great deal worse than marry such a clever, pretty girl even if she was only a miller's daughter.

"Now," thought the girl, as soon as the King had left her, "I must wait patiently for my little friend. Surely he will come."

She sat down on the stool provided for her and clasped her hands in her lap. Then she began to count, "One, two, three, four . . ."

When she reached twenty the door suddenly opened and in came the little goblin. "What will you give me," he asked, "if I once again spin all this straw into gold?"

Now the girl's eyes clouded. What could she give the little man? She had given him her necklace and her ring and she had nothing else to give.

"I – I am sorry," she stammered. "I have nothing to give you this time. But won't you wait until I am the Queen – ah, then you can have any treasure you ask for!"

"You must give me your first-born child," said the dwarf. "Promise that you will give me your first-born and I will spin the straw into gold for you."

"I promise!" cried the girl. "I promise – but please set to work at once for there is twice as much straw as before."

The little man sat down at the wheel, and in a few minutes the shuttle was full. Then he filled another and another and another until, by daybreak, he had spun all the straw into shining gold.

The King was so delighted at the sight of the gold that he declared he would marry the miller's daughter that same day. The wedding, though arranged in such haste, was a grand affair.

A year afterwards, the Queen gave birth to a fine baby boy. Of

course, she had forgotten all about the goblin who had saved her and the promise she had made to him. So imagine her surprise and horror when one day, as she was sitting nursing her baby, he suddenly came into her room.

"Give me the child," he demanded.

"I cannot do such a terrible thing!" cried the young Queen in deep distress. "You may have my jewels, my golden crown, any-thing – but not my baby!"

"I want only your child," said the little man.

At this the girl, quite forgetting her queenly dignity, dropped to her knees and begged the dwarf to change his mind. So piteously did she plead that, at last, he said, "I will give you three days to discover my name. If you can you may keep your son."

When the goblin had gone, the Queen immediately sent out her most trusted messengers to far corners of the kingdom to enquire in all the towns and cities about unusual names. They came back with names like Jasper and Crispin and Melchior.

"I will try them on the little man when he comes next," she said.

Next morning the goblin once more appeared before her and she began, "Your name is Jasper!"

"It is not," replied the dwarf and he grinned from ear to ear.

"Then it is Crispin – or – or Melchior."

"No, no, it is not!" he replied again, even more delighted.

The Queen tried to hide her dismay. "Come again tomorrow," she said. "Tomorrow I will know."

This time the messengers went further afield to the villages and hamlets and small out-of-the-way farms. And when the dwarf came the next day, the Queen was ready for him with a whole string of unusual names.

"It must be Baltimore or Jude," she said.

"No, it is not Baltimore, nor is it Jude," chuckled the goblin.

"Then it is Finnegan!" cried the Queen.

"No, no it is not!" said the dwarf, clapping his hands in glee. "Tomorrow is your last chance. Then the child will be mine."

Alone again the Queen gave way to bitter tears. But soon she pulled herself together and thought what she must do. Then she summoned one of her most trusted servants. "Take a horse and make for the hills," she said. "And whenever you meet a stranger, enquire of him what he calls his son. Ride until your horse is too weary to continue. But be sure to return to me by early morning."

When the messenger returned he came straight to the Queen. It looked at first as if he had had no luck.

"I could not find a single new name," he admitted. "But something strange happened. My horse fell lame so I dismounted and climbed to the top of a high mountain. There right on the very top was a little house."

"Did you see anyone?" asked the Queen. "Did anyone live in the little house?"

"There was a fire burning in front of it," the messenger replied, "and, as I watched from behind a rock, I saw the oddest little creature come out and begin hopping and prancing around the fire. Then he began to sing – such a strange, cracked voice he had! It made me take note of the words."

"The words – what were the words?" demanded the Queen.

"Strange words indeed, Your Majesty," said the messenger.
"Today I bake, tomorrow I brew
The next I'll have the young Queen's child
Ho! glad am I that no one knew
That Rumpelstiltskin I am styled."

"That's the name then!" cried the Queen, and in her excitement she took off her diamond necklace and gave it to the astonished messenger. Then, composing herself, she sat down to await the dwarf.

No sooner did he come than she began, "Is your name Ruben?"

"No," he said, already beginning to smile.

"What about Conrad?"

The little man shook his head, his eyes bright with triumph.

"Then – then perhaps it is Rumpelstiltskin!"

At the sound of his name, the little man's expression changed to one of terrible rage. He stamped the floor so hard with his foot that he disappeared forever into the hole he had made in the floor.

Jack the Giant Killer

THIS MAY be true or it may not, but it is commonly believed that a boy named Jack was the most famous killer of giants who has ever lived.

Jack was the son of a wealthy Cornish farmer who lived close to Land's End in England. Now, in the reign of King Arthur, the country was sorely afflicted by a monstrous giant, who was very, very tall and very, very round. His home was a cave on the Mount of Cornwall. This giant had a wicked and ugly face which struck terror into the few who had glimpsed it, and so evil was his reputation that no man, even those noted for their bravery, would volunteer to approach his cave.

Jack had often listened to the horrifying tales of the giant's activities; how he killed men and ate them; how he stole the farmers' cattle by the hundreds, and how, stored up in his vast cave, was a treasure worth a King's ransom.

One day Jack and his father were summoned to the Town Hall to attend a meeting about the giant and to discuss what could be done, for life was becoming unbearable for the people of the area.

"And what kind of reward could the hero who tackles this dreadful giant expect to be given?" asked Jack, after a long discussion which had really gotten nobody anywhere.

"Ah-ha," said the Town Clerk. "That's a good question. I vote that anyone who kills the giant takes all his treasure for his own."

"That would certainly be reward enough for me!" cried Jack. "I'm your man! I will rid you of this terrible giant."

Well, Jack, who was as quick-witted and clever as he was brave, collected together a pickaxe, a shovel and a horn, and the very next day, he set out for the Cornish Mount. It was winter and the days were short but Jack traveled at a good pace and reached the Mount just as it was growing dark.

Halfway up the steep hill, Jack sat down to rest and before long he heard the giant's loud snores. Satisfied that the monster would not easily be disturbed, Jack took his pickaxe and his shovel and began to work. He worked all through the night, digging and shoveling until he had made a huge pit, which was both extremely deep and extremely wide. This he covered with straw and long sticks and over these he scattered earth so that it looked just like ordinary ground.

Now this pit, as you have probably guessed, was pretty close to the giant's cave. In fact it was just outside it. Jack took up a position on the far side of it so that if the giant made a rush at him he would go crashing into the hole.

When Jack was completely satisfied with his labors, he unslung his horn, put it to his mouth and blew a long shrill blast.

In an instant the giant came stumbling out of his cave in a terrible rage, shouting, "You worm! Wake me from my slumbers, would you? Why I'll have you for breakfast!" He lumbered forward – and tumbled straight into the pit with such a crashing thud that it shook the whole Mount.

"So you would have me for breakfast, eh!" little Jack cried, looking down at the trapped giant. "I think not! For this is the end of you and your wicked deeds."

And he aimed a hefty blow with his pickaxe at the giant's head which killed him on the spot.

Then Jack ran into the cave and there found treasure enough to make a whole town rich. So he was well rewarded for his bravery.

But the townspeople, when they heard that the giant was dead, were so grateful to Jack that they collected a vast sum of money and

presented their hero with a fine sword and a silver belt on which the words "Jack the Giant Killer" were embroidered in letters of gold.

You might imagine that Jack would settle down on his father's farm and be content. But not so! His mind was full of giants and when, one day, his father sent him on a journey to Wales to purchase some sheep, Jack was pleased beyond measure to hear about another giant. This one was an extra challenge, as he was also a magician and he lived in an enchanted castle in a forest.

Jack journeyed into the forest for some way. Then, feeling tired, he sat down under a tree and was soon fast asleep. As he slept, who should come striding along but the giant himself! And it didn't take him long to realize that he had every giant's sworn enemy in his power for, of course, Jack was wearing his silver belt with the words "Jack the Giant Killer" embroidered on it.

Well, the giant scooped Jack up in his hands with much the same ease as you and I would pick up a pebble and marched off with him to his enchanted castle. When Jack woke up he found himself a long way up from the ground and passing across the castle's courtyard. All around were strewn the bones of the giant's victims.

"It won't be long before your bones join these others," the giant laughed spitefully, as he entered the castle and climbed up to one of the turret rooms. "But in the meantime you'll be safe enough in here," he added, as he dropped Jack onto the floor.

For the first time in his life Jack was really afraid and he grew all the more so when he heard the most melancholy wailings and shrieks which he guessed came from the giant's other captives.

He ran to the window and saw the giant at the castle gates in conversation with another of his fellows, who was every bit as horrible to look at.

"No doubt he is inviting him to breakfast on my remains," Jack thought to himself grimly. And then as the two giants began to walk slowly towards the castle – deep in conversation – Jack had a brilliant idea.

In a corner of his turret he had discovered two lengths of strong cord. He took hold of them testing their strength, and then he made a noose at the end of each of them. He had only just time to take up his position at the window before the giants passed directly beneath him. Straightaway he let the nooses fall around their necks.

Before the two astonished giants had a chance to realize what was happening, Jack threw the other ends of the ropes over a strong beam and pulled with all his might. As the nooses tightened around their necks, the giants went black in the face. Within a minute they had lost their senses, so Jack slid down the rope and slew them both.

Then he took the castle keys and opened all the dungeon doors, setting free a number of beautiful maidens, who fell upon his neck with cries of gratitude. Jack sent them on their way back to their own homes and then, well pleased with his day's work, resumed his journey into Wales.

By nightfall, however, he had lost his way and found himself passing through a lonely valley. There were no houses to be seen except one large gray stone mansion. Tired and weary, he went up to it and knocked on the door.

To his astonishment the door was opened almost at once by the most awful fellow he had yet seen; a two-headed giant!

Now this giant was a Welsh giant and had a reputation for cunning rather than cattle-eating. Still he was a giant and Jack guessed that he would not easily escape from his clutches.

The giant offered him a night's shelter which Jack accepted. But he did not trust his smiling host and instead of sleeping on the bed, he stuffed his pillows with logs and then hid underneath the bed. It was just as well he had taken this precaution for, in the middle of the night, in came the giant and thumped at the pillows with his club.

The giant was amazed when Jack appeared for breakfast the next morning, but he hid his surprise as well as he could and offered Jack an enormous bowl of cold porridge.

"You'll manage that easily after your long journey," he said.

"Of course I will," said Jack. But when the giant was busy eating he managed to tip most of the cold porridge into the leather pouch he carried round his waist.

Now the giant was hoping that Jack would be so sleepy after eating such a huge amount of food that he would be able to do what he liked with him. But, of course, Jack was as merry as a cricket.

"I'll show you a trick," he said to the giant. "It's one you will never be able to do."

And he took a knife and ripped open the leather pouch which was hidden under his coat. Out tumbled all the cold porridge and fell onto the floor.

"A grasshopper like you is not going to get the better of me!" cried the giant, who was a conceited fellow. "What you can do – I can do!" And seizing the knife, he killed himself on the spot!

Jack was delighted that he had rid the world of yet another giant.

He found his way out of the lonely valley and journeyed to the market town where he was to purchase the sheep for his father. This done, he returned home and was content to stay there for some months. But he had acquired such a taste for adventure that soon he determined to leave the farm once again.

First, he went to a friendly magician whose daughter he had released from the enchanted castle and who owed him a favor.

The magician was only too glad to oblige and he gave Jack a horse that could travel swifter than the wind, together with a magic sword and a coat that would make him invisible when he put it on.

Armed with these magnificent gifts, Jack set out to find and destroy the remaining giants in his part of the world. He rode over endless countryside until he came, at last, to a great forest. He hadn't traveled far among the dark trees before he saw a truly monstrous giant. The monster, who was almost as wide as he was tall, was dragging a knight and his fair lady along by the hair.

The lady was begging pathetically for mercy, but the giant merely laughed and told her that he was taking her back to his den for his evening meal!

On hearing this, Jack jumped down from his horse, put on his invisible coat, and drew his magic sword. As there was no possible way he could kill the enormous giant outright, he decided to begin by cutting off his legs – an act which in itself took all his strength. Then Jack used his special magic sword to cut off the giant's head.

The knight and his lady wanted to take him to their home and

shower him with gifts but Jack politely refused their hospitality. "I have sworn," he told them, "not to rest until I have done away with all such monsters as the one who captured you. And besides I must find out where this dead giant lived for he may have other gentle folk as his prisoners."

So Jack rode on through the forest and though he missed the giant's den completely, he did come upon a lonely house standing at the foot of a steep mountain.

An old man was walking in the garden and Jack asked him why he looked so sad.

"I mourn the loss of my master the Duke's beautiful daughter," said the old man. "She has been captured by a terrible giant, by the name of Galligantua, who lives in an enchanted castle at the very top of this high mountain."

"You are talking to the right man if you are seeking help to overthrow the giant," said Jack, pointing to his belt.

"Then I am right glad to see you," said the old servant. "But it would not be fair to let you think that you have only the giant to fight. His closest companion is a wizard of great power and cunning – a most evil person. It was he who changed the Duke's daughter into a deer."

Jack could scarcely wait for the old man to finish his woeful tale. But as soon as he had heard the words he ran out of the garden and began immediately to climb the mountain. When he reached the top, he found himself in front of the giant's castle, the entrance of which was guarded by a pair of fire-eating dragons. He passed them easily enough, however, by putting on his invisible coat. Once inside the courtyard he read the words engraved on a tablet of stone.

"Whoever can this trumpet blow
Shall soon Galligantua overthrow."

Beside the tablet was a golden trumpet. Jack seized it and put it to his lips and the shrill blast he blew on it made the castle shiver to its foundations. At once all the doors flew open, and with a triumphant shout Jack entered the castle. He found the giant and the wizard seated at a table in the vast dining hall. And, made completely invisible by his cloak, Jack was able to cut off their heads without any fuss or bother.

The wizard's death broke the spell which had kept a number of lords and ladies imprisoned in the shape of various beasts. The kittens and cats quickly changed into beautiful-looking young ladies. The Duke's daughter, however, having only recently been captured was in a separate part of the castle and Jack did not rest until he had found her.

Then Jack conducted the lords and ladies and the Duke's daughter down the mountainside and saw to it that they were all able to find their own way home. But the Duke's daughter he kept by his side as long as possible for she was very beautiful as well as being very loving and gentle in her manner towards him.

Now, you may be sure, in a very short time Jack's reputation as a killer of giants reached the ears of King Arthur. And he was particularly pleased to learn of the end of the monster, Galligantua. He was so pleased in fact that he sent for Jack.

"I would like to reward you for your bravery," said the monarch. "Ask any favor you like and it shall be granted."

Jack did not need to think for long. "I would like the Duke's daughter as my bride, Your Majesty," he said.

"And that is what I thought you might say," said King Arthur, who was a romantic and understanding sovereign. "It was she who told me something of your deeds."

Well, it wasn't long before Jack and the lovely lady were happily married and, thanks to the King's generosity, were most comfortably settled in a grand house surrounded by fields and woods.

There is no record to say whether or not Jack went out giant-hunting after he was married, but most people think that in fact he stayed at home to take care of his estates and to keep his gentle wife happy for the rest of their days.

The Brother and the Sister

ONCE UPON a time a brother and a sister, who were the very best of friends, lived happily together with their mother and father. Alas, when the mother died their father married again – not realizing that his new wife was none other than a wicked, evil witch. From the time she first came into the house, she was determined to get rid of the children.

She began by feeding them on stale crusts of bread and dressing them in rags. Then as soon as their father left to go to work she would beat them cruelly. This unhappy state of affairs continued for quite some time until, finally one day, the children could stand it no longer.

"Our stepmother must be a witch, a wicked witch," said the brother. "If we stay here any longer she will find a way to really do us harm. We must run away."

So, as dawn broke the next day, they left home. All day, they journeyed through meadows and fields until at last they came to a great forest.

"We could live here," said the sister, who was getting tired.

"What do you think, Brother? The witch will never find us here."

But there the girl was wrong for the witch possessed strong magical powers. When the brother went off in search of a stream, the witch – hidden from sight – was not far behind him.

As the boy bent down to drink, his gentle sister heard a voice from the stream saying, "Whoever drinks my waters will become a tiger; drink me and become a tiger."

"Stop! Don't drink!" the sister cried desperately. "Brother, the stream is our friend, but our wicked stepmother must have bewitched it! Did you not hear its warning? If you drink, you will turn into a tiger."

The boy was very thirsty, but he could not bear to see his sister in such distress. "I won't drink its waters," he assured her. "Why, if I became a tiger, I might eat you!"

Now this was exactly what the witch had hoped would happen when she had cast her spell upon the stream. Her red eyes glowed with anger as she watched the boy stand up without drinking.

"Come, let's go on through the forest," he said, taking his sister's hand. "I will find another stream and drink from that instead."

But when they did find another stream and the boy once again bent down, his sister heard a voice saying, "Whoever drinks my waters will become a wolf; drink me and become a wolf!"

And once again she cried out in terror, "Brother, Brother, you must not drink. Our wicked stepmother cannot be far behind us, for she has cast her spell upon this stream too."

When the witch, who was hiding behind a bush, heard the girl's warning, she gnashed her teeth in rage. Furious and revengeful, she followed the brother and sister as they walked on.

"Sister, I must drink at the next stream," the boy said after a while. "I am dying of thirst."

His sister trembled as he spoke, for she was certain that the wicked witch was still somewhere in the forest, probably quite close to them. And when the sound of water rippling over stones told her that they were once again close to a stream, she clutched her brother's arm.

But the boy shook himself free and ran ahead to the stream.

"Wait, wait for me," cried the girl and ran after him.

As he bent down to drink, she heard the voice of the stream saying, "Whoever drinks my waters will become a fawn; drink me and become a fawn."

"Brother, Brother, do not drink," the girl pleaded. "If you do you will become a fawn and run away from me. Then I shall be all alone in this forest with no one to protect me."

This time, her brother would not listen. He was so thirsty that he could think only of the cool, refreshing water. But as soon as he began to drink, he changed into a soft, brown fawn. As he did so, the sister heard an evil, cackling laugh fill the air.

The sister wept when she saw her poor brother standing in front of her in the shape of a fawn, and the fawn wept too, as he stood, powerless to do anything.

"I cannot undo our stepmother's spell," the sister whispered at last. "But we can stay together. I will never leave you and you must never leave me." And she took off her golden garter and put it round the fawn's neck; then she made a soft rope of some rushes and fastened it to the garter. Now she could lead the fawn and keep him close to her as they went deeper into the forest.

That night, when it was nearly dark, the girl found a little hut. When she peeped inside and it was empty, for the first time that day a smile lit up her sweet face.

"We have found a home, Brother," she said almost gaily. "You

stay here while I find some leaves and moss for your bed and gather
roots and berries and nuts for our supper. I think we should stay
here for as long as we can."

The brother and sister stayed for some years in the forest. Often
the girl would feel great sadness as she looked at her brother, and
she wished with all her heart that she could change him back into his
human form. But she always pretended to be happy when she was
with him. She played with him outside their hut and found him the
greenest grass to eat. And at night, she slept with her head on his
back, drawing comfort from his nearness and soft warmth.

One day the young King of the country came to the forest to
hunt. He brought with him a great troop of men and dogs and
before long the sound of the hunting horns and barking came to the
ears of the brother and sister.

The fawn pawed the ground and raised his head eagerly, but
straightaway the girl threw her arms around his neck. "No, no,
Brother," she cried anxiously. "You must not join in the hunt.
Then men will shoot at you and the dogs will pull you down."

But the fawn could not stay still just as long as he could hear the
horns. "I must run free in the forest today," he told his sister. "Do

not stop me!" And he looked so pitiful and yet so eager to be free that his sister agreed to let him go.

"But promise to come back to me when night falls," she said. "I shall shut and bolt the door against the hunters. But when you come I shall let you in. Be sure and use the words, 'My Sister, let me in,' so that I shall know it is you."

The fawn promised that he would return at nightfall and use the words she had told him. Then he bounded joyfully away into the forest and was soon lost to the gentle girl's sight. All that day he encouraged the hunters and the dogs to chase after him but he was so fast that he outran them all. That night, as darkness fell, he returned to the hut and knocked gently on the door, crying, "My Sister, let me in."

His sister unbolted the door and put her arms round his neck in loving welcome before giving him his supper.

Early the next morning the sound of the horns echoed again through the forest. Once more the fawn raised his head eagerly and once more his sister pleaded with him not to go. But, in spite of her protestations, the fawn could not remain indoors while the hunters were in the forest.

"Be very careful," she warned finally, as she opened the door.

That day the hunters, with the King at their head, got closer to the fawn, even wounding him slightly, but still they could not capture him. The King vowed he would not give up the chase.

When the fawn returned to the hut and the sister saw he was hurt, she was very frightened. "I will dress your wound with herbs," she told him, "and as it is not too severe, it will soon heal. But now I beg you, do not go out again."

But the fawn could not promise truthfully and in the morning, as the horns sounded, his sister saw that he meant to go out.

"Take care then, dear Brother," she whispered, as she opened the door to let him free.

Now the King had grown curious about this fawn with its enticing ways and its golden collar, and that day he asked his huntsmen if any of them knew where the animal went at night.

"I know, sire," said one of the men. "Last night I saw the fawn knock on the door of a little hut deep in the forest and I heard him say, 'My Sister, let me in.'"

"Indeed," said the King, greatly interested. "And did someone let the animal in?"

"Yes, Your Majesty," replied the huntsman. "A most beautiful young girl. She opened the door and the fawn disappeared inside."

Then the King gave orders that the fawn should not be harmed that day, no matter how close the huntsmen were able to get to him. And just as darkness began to fall, he himself went along to the hut, having been shown its whereabouts by his huntsman. As he knocked on the door, he said softly, "My Sister, let me in." Almost at once the door was opened.

So lovely was the girl who stood before him that the King bowed and kissed her hand.

"I have searched long for such a one as you," he said. "Come to my palace with me, and I will make you my Queen."

Before she could get over the shock of seeing the young King at the door of the hut that had become their home, the fawn came leaping in. The King looked on as the girl ran to the animal and put her arms around his neck.

"Yes, yes, I will come with you to your palace," she cried, looking up at the King, "and be your loving wife – if only I may keep my brother the fawn safe. He must come with me."

The King was only too happy to grant her request, and so the brother and sister left the hut in the forest and went to live in the King's great palace.

The fawn was content to run free in the palace gardens and to see the happiness in his sister's face after she was married. There was joy everywhere in the palace, for very soon the Queen had won the hearts of all those who served her.

All might have been well if news of the beautiful young Queen and the fawn she called 'Brother,' had not reached the ears of the wicked stepmother. For a long time now she had been sure that the fawn had been killed and the girl had died of a broken heart. You can imagine how angry and jealous she felt when she learned the truth! To make matters even worse her only daughter, who had only one eye and was dreadfully ugly, took to reproaching the evil witch bitterly.

"And to think that she should end up a Queen while I remain here," the witch's daughter would mutter over and over again. "That is too much to bear!"

"If only you will wait patiently," the old woman told her, "I will take my revenge, you'll see. My heart is too full of bitter hatred to let me rest until I have destroyed her and her miserable 'brother'!"

The witch used her evil powers to receive news of all that took place in the palace each day. At last she learned that the Queen had given birth to an enchanting baby boy.

"My chance has come," she told her ugly daughter, gleefully. "Now I am going to the palace."

Then the witch changed herself into a pleasant-looking serving-woman and presented herself at the palace. She was taken on as chambermaid to the Queen, who was ill in bed after the birth of her son and required careful nursing until her strength returned.

As soon as the "chambermaid" was allowed to move freely in and out of the young Queen's bedroom, she sent for her daughter. And together they plotted how they might destroy the Queen.

"When next she takes her bath," said the witch at last, "you must help me to carry her into the bathroom. We will make up a fire so that it is very hot. Then we will close all the windows and the door, and our pretty mistress will suffocate."

This was done, and no one in the palace guessed the fate of their Queen, for the old witch dressed her daughter in the royal robes and gave her the shape and form of the lovely young woman. She could not, however, give her two eyes, but the hood, which she told

her to wear, all but covered her face. Then she drew the heavy brocade curtains around the bed and waited for the King to arrive.

He came at last eager to greet his young wife, but the chambermaid told him that her mistress must not be disturbed and that she was sleeping soundly. Disappointed, the King went away.

At midnight, when all in the palace were sleeping except the royal baby's nurse who was constantly by the cradle, the real Queen came noiselessly into the room. She glided over to the cradle, picked up her little son and caressed him for a while. Kissing him softly, she put him back in his cot and moved over to where the fawn lay in his corner. Gently, she stroked his head and then without a word she disappeared through the door.

This happened for a number of nights and the nurse grew more and more puzzled at what she thought was a ghostly vision. At last she told the King.

"This is very strange," he said thoughtfully. "It is also very strange that my dear wife will not permit me to go near her bed."

"Your Majesty," suggested the nurse timidly, "why do you not hide yourself in the nursery so that you can find out the truth?"

"That is my intention," said the King, nodding his head.

As he waited anxiously that same night for the "vision" to appear, he thought only of his love for his Queen and their son. Then as the clock began to strike midnight, his wife glided silently into the room. The King saw her gather the child into her arms and heard her murmur softly.

"How does my babe? How does my fawn?

I come this once, but nevermore."

"Why do you ask?" he cried, springing from his hiding place and putting his arms about her. "That girl in your bed – who is she?"

Then the Queen, as the King kissed her tenderly, was miraculously restored to life. She told her husband the whole sad story of how the wicked witch and her daughter had taken the life which was now given back to her.

"They shall both get the punishment they deserve," vowed the King, trembling with anger. Immediately he summoned the Guard and told them to seize the two evil-doers.

Taken by surprise, the witch had no time to cast any of her spells. Her hateful daughter was carried off into the forest to be devoured by wild beasts, while the witch was thrown into a great fire that had been built in the courtyard.

When all that was left of the witch was a handful of ashes, the spell, which had for so long bound the Queen's brother, was broken. The fawn changed into a handsome young man. Joyfully, the brother and sister embraced each other, and the King promised, as he had promised long ago in the forest, that the two should remain together for as long as they wanted.

Hans and the Little Iron Man

YOU MIGHT think that every King is happy, for Kings have all the money in the world to spend. They have the finest of horses to ride, the most precious jewels to wear and the grandest of palaces in which to live. But there was once a King who had all these things and yet was far from happy. In fact, he was very unhappy and it was all because of his daughter. She was very beautiful, but she lay in bed, dull and lifeless, suffering from a mysterious illness which no one could cure.

The King grew more and more unhappy as he looked at his lovely child lying helplessly in bed. Doctors from all over the world came to examine her and they all prescribed different cures, but none – it seemed – were the slightest bit of use.

At last, one wise old man of medicine, who had traveled a very long way to see the sick Princess, gave his opinion.

"Your daughter will get well," he said, "if she eats a particular kind of apple."

Now the King was not quite sure if he should take the doctor's advice seriously but, nevertheless, he sent out a proclamation,

which had soon been read throughout his kingdom. It said that whosoever brought his daughter an apple, which when she ate it made her well again, should have her as his wife and be King.

The King's proclamation was talked about everywhere and so it wasn't long before a poor peasant-farmer heard of it. He made up his mind straightaway to send some of his own home-grown apples to the palace.

Very excited, he called his three sons together after supper.

"You must be the one to take my apples," he told the eldest. "They are such splendid, rosy-red apples that they are sure to make the Princess well again. Then the King will keep his promise and allow you to marry her."

"I'd like that," said the eldest son. "I'd like to marry a real Princess." And his handsome face lit up at the very idea. Then he added, "And I'd like all the power and the glory of being a King, too. Why I'd soon show them at the palace who was the master!"

Early the next morning he went out into the orchard and filled a basket with his father's choicest apples. Then he set out for the palace. He had not gone very far down the road when he met a little iron man, whose dwarf-like stature and ugly face made the handsome youth look down on him quite scornfully.

"What have you got in your basket?" asked the little man.

Straightaway the youth replied, "That's no business of yours — frogs' legs!" Then he hurried on.

"Well, so shall it be, and so shall it remain," uttered the dwarf, as he turned aside.

When the farmer's eldest son arrived at the palace he quickly let it be known that he had brought apples which would certainly make the Princess well again. And when the King heard news of this he was so pleased and delighted he ordered the youth to be brought to him immediately.

Alas, when the young man stood in front of the King and removed the cover from his basket there were no lovely rosy apples to be seen. Instead the basket was full of frogs' legs, and they were still kicking about too!

"Take them away," ordered the King, furious and disappointed. "And throw this young impostor into the street."

When the farmer heard what had happened on his eldest son's return, he went out into his orchard the next morning and gathered the choicest apples himself. Then he carefully put them into the basket.

"You take the basket this time," he said, giving it to his second

son. "And don't linger on the way but make straight for the palace."

"I'm sure to be lucky," said the second son, confidently. He was secretly pleased that his brother had failed. "I'll soon be sending you news from the palace that I have won both a Princess and a kingdom!"

Dressed in his best jacket and breeches, he was soon on the road to the palace with his basket of apples. He had not gone far, however, when he also met the little iron dwarf.

"What have you got in your basket?" asked the dwarf of him. And the young man retorted impatiently, "What's that to you — hogs' bristles!" And he pushed him roughly out of his way.

"Well, so shall it be, and so shall it remain," muttered the dwarf, as he turned aside.

When he reached the palace, the farmer's second son shouted loudly for servants to take him to the King. This time the guards were a little slower in letting him pass. "His Majesty was furious with the fellow who brought him frogs' legs instead of apples only yesterday," they said. "Are you sure your basket contains apples?"

"Of course I am," the youth protested. "They are the finest apples in the land and there will be trouble if you don't let me take them to the King."

So the guards allowed him to pass and presently he found himself standing in front of the King.

"Show me your apples," the King ordered sternly.

But when the youth uncovered the basket there were no lovely rosy-red apples inside – only hogs' bristles. The King was so angry at the sight of them that he had the youth whipped out of the palace.

The farmer was terribly upset when his second son arrived home with his best suit all torn and his face scratched.

And when he had heard the story for the tenth time, he said, "Well, I have no more sons to send so we had best forget the whole sorry business."

"You have me!" said Hans, the youngest, who was always pushed into the background by his father and brothers.

"If my two handsome, clever sons fail, there can be no chance for a stupid lad like you," said his father angrily. "So be quiet and get on with your work,"

"But I would like to go," pleaded Hans. "What does it matter if I do fail? It will give you all a chance to laugh at me. Please, Father, let me take some of your apples to the palace."

"Oh let him try," said the second son, irritably. Then he added spitefully, "And I hope they set the dogs on him – then I will think I escaped lightly!"

"I'm sorry you got a whipping," said Hans. And he really meant it for he had a kind heart and a sunny nature which kept him cheerful in spite of all the hard work he had to do.

"Very well then," said the old man at last. "Pick your own apples and go to the palace tomorrow with them. But don't waste time; we need you to clean out the stables."

Hans was up early the next morning and was soon on the road with his basket of apples. Almost at once he met the shabby little dwarf in his iron clothes.

"What have you got in the basket?" asked the little man just as he had of Hans' brothers.

And, smiling, Hans told him about the apples and why he was taking them to the palace.

"Wouldn't it be wonderful if they did cure the poor Princess!" he exclaimed at last. "I – dreamt of Princesses last night!" he added shyly and laughed.

The dwarf laughed in sympathy; then he said, "So shall they be, and so shall they remain," before turning aside.

But it was no easy job for Hans to get into the palace as the guards were now very suspicious. "Two men have succeeded in fooling us and the King already," one of the guards told him. "If you are trying to deceive us then you had better admit it now. We're not fools you know!"

"My basket contains nothing but apples," said Hans, and he tried to lift the cover. But the soldier stopped him.

"You have an honest face," said he. "And a pleasant manner – not like the other two rascals who were here before you. Go on – you are free to enter the palace."

When Hans at last stood before the King and pulled the cover away, there sat in his basket, not the rosy-red apples he had expected to see, but the most wonderful golden-yellow apples, which looked almost too good to eat.

"Take them to my daughter at once," the excited King said immediately to one of his servants. "And you wait here, young man, until she has had time to eat one."

Hans waited nervously – the minutes seeming like hours. At last the doors opened and who should walk in but the Princess herself. She was completely recovered!

The King was so happy at the sight of his pretty daughter's

smiling face that he almost forgot about Hans. When he did remember, he turned to him and said, "The Princess is cured, and I am grateful, I assure you. I will see you are richly rewarded."

"But – but you promised that . . ." Hans stammered, his heart sinking.

"Ah, yes, but . . ." interrupted the King, rather disturbed as he remembered what the reward was to be. Then he repeated, "Ah, yes, but . . ." once again to give himself time to think. "Well, there is a task which must be undertaken before you can be King and marry my daughter. You must make a boat which goes as well on land as it does on the sea."

"Very well," said Hans. "I'll go back home and see to it."

As soon as he had returned home, Hans told his father and brothers all that had taken place at the palace.

"You are not clever enough to make such a boat," declared his father impatiently. "Now your eldest brother is different. He shall go into the forest and set to work immediately. Then he can sail the boat back to the palace."

Hans' eldest brother went into the forest that same day and worked hard on the boat. When it was half built, the same little iron man he had met on the road suddenly appeared.

"What are you making?" he asked.

"None of your business – wooden bowls for the kitchen!" replied the youth, sneering as he spoke.

And the dwarf said quietly, "So it shall be, and so it shall remain." And he vanished.

Just as it was growing dark, the young man finished the boat and, whistling cheerfully, he returned home, thinking he would go to the palace the next day. But in the morning, when he went to sail it, all he found was a heap of wooden bowls.

Somewhat annoyed, the farmer sent his second son into the forest, but everything went with him just as it had done with his brother.

So now it was Hans' turn once more. He worked so hard at his boat that he was soon tired and hot but still he managed to sing a merry tune as he swung his axe.

In the middle of the day, the little man appeared and asked him what he was making.

"I'm making a boat," Hans told him. "A wonderful, wonderful boat that will move faster over dry land than it will sail on the sea. I'm taking it to the palace so that I can win the King's daughter and be King."

"Good," said the dwarf. "So it shall be, and so it shall remain." And once more he vanished straightaway.

Hans worked long and hard all day, and in the evening, when the sun was setting, his boat was finished. Straightaway he jumped into it and rowed to the palace. The boat traveled as swiftly as the wind, and the King, looking out of one of his windows, saw it coming. He was surprised and annoyed, but now he had had time to think up another task for Hans and so save his daughter from marrying a common peasant boy.

"You have done well," he said, when Hans arrived in the wonderful boat. "But before you claim your reward you must take a hundred hares out to pasture in the royal meadow and keep them there from early morning to late at night. If one escapes you, you shall not have the Princess."

Early the next morning Hans went to the royal meadow with the hundred hares and set them free to graze. This time he was more than a little worried for he could not imagine how he could stop them from running away. He was lucky though and once again his funny little friend, the iron man, suddenly appeared before him.

"What are you doing?" he asked.

And Hans told him how he must keep all the hares together in the meadow and not lose one of them.

"Easy enough," said the dwarf. "Here is a whistle for you. If one runs away, the sound of the whistle will bring it back."

Hans took the whistle gratefully, and the little man vanished. Now Hans' task was simple – a single note on the whistle and the hares would gather about him obediently. Whenever one looked like running away, the whistle brought it back again.

As Hans sat watching his hundred hares and thinking about the little iron man he saw the King's beautiful daughter coming towards him.

She moved with such grace that his heart turned over and he thought, "There is no other girl in the world as lovely as the Princess! And to think she will soon be mine!"

And the Princess, as she faced Hans, thought, "My father is right – he is nothing but a common farmer's boy, but how handsome he looks today. What a merry smile he has!"

But being a King's daughter, the girl hid her feelings and her voice was cold and hard when she spoke. "My father," she said, "has sent me for one of the hares. He is about to entertain an important guest who has expressed the wish for hare soup. Give me one immediately."

"I cannot do that," said Hans mildly.

"You must!" insisted the Princess haughtily. And she stamped

her little foot. "You must do what my father says and, besides," she added in a softer voice, "it is my wish too."

Hans shook his head, but he was already so much in love with the Princess that he could not bring himself to deny her anything.

"Oh, very well," he said at last. "I know that it is a trick – for once you take the hare back to the royal kitchens I will be left with only ninety-nine."

The Princess studied her feet, not wishing to meet Hans' honest eyes, for she too knew that it was a trick thought up by her father. She held out her dainty apron and Hans caught up one of the hares and put it there.

Without a word of thanks she turned away and Hans watched her go. "Now I have lost not only the hare but a Princess and a kingdom as well," he said to himself. "Or have I?" For he had suddenly remembered his magic whistle.

He took it out and blew upon it – one short, sharp blast. Instantly the hare jumped out of the girl's apron and, though she chased after it, it was much too fast for her and was soon back with the herd.

"I will not ask you for another," she said with the flicker of a smile. "But my father will not be at all pleased."

As darkness fell, Hans drove all the hares back to the palace and not a single one was missing.

You wouldn't think that a King would dare to break his royal word a third time, would you? But this King did! He had all the hares counted – not once but six times over. And when his Lord High Chancellor assured him that there were one hundred hares, all present and correct, and that it was his opinion that counting them for the seventh time would make no difference, the King was not at all pleased. In fact he was furious.

"Why not send him to the man-eating Griffin?" suggested the Chancellor. "Tell him you want one of the Griffin's feathers."

"That's a very good idea," said the King. And he told Hans that if he managed to bring back one of the Griffin's feathers then he could marry his daughter and have the kingdom for his own.

Without a word of reproach, Hans set off for the Griffin's lair. Happily, luck was with him all the way there, and all the way back, for not only did he obtain one of the fierce Griffin's feathers but he won for himself a fortune in gold and silver.

Was it the sight of all the gold and silver that made the King fulfill his promise at last? Or was it the whispered conversation he held with his daughter while Hans stood before them? Well, we shall never know! But before the week was out Hans and the Princess were married. A thousand guests were invited to the ceremony, and Hans was more than delighted to see his two brothers and his father among them. But there was one other guest for whom he searched in vain. The little iron man!

"I'm sure to meet up with him one day," Hans told himself as he went back to his Princess. "And when I do, I shall make his fortune, just as he has made mine!"